Hunter and the Easter Bunny

By Charlotte Cherry

This is a story about one of the greatest heroes of our time. You will probably know him as 'The Easter Bunny'. He is a magical giant rabbit whom is never seen yet always welcome. A big brown rabbit with huge googly eyes. Such a kind and fun creature that everyone likes and wants to cuddle. Every year he works at creating chocolate eggs and delivers them to all the little boys and girls throughout the world. He is nothing more and nothing less than an angelic chocolate giving god.

However, this one year something bad happened..... The Easter Bunny was mixing up some more chocolate at his factory which was situated well underneath the ground. All of a sudden there was a loud bang and the chocolate machine ground to a halt. It was broken!

The Easter Bunny heard the noise and jumped into the large pool of delicious chocolate to try and find the problem. On inspection he found that a large nut had become stuck in one of the chocolifiers and he tried and tried to dislodge it. Finally he did but he caught his leg and crack!!

Once the Easter Bunny was dragged out of the chocolifiers by the Easter Chick Doctors they laid him out and had worried looks on their yellow faces. Yes, unfortunately the leg was broken and he was going to need complete rest. It was nothing short of a disaster and for the first time ever it seemed that Easter would have to be cancelled. Everyone looked upset and didn't know what to do.

"I have an idea" said the Easter Bunny. Bring me the ChoccoKidApp. Two obedient Easter Chicks brought in an electronic gadget that had a display and a giant red button. This device was normally used for determining who was next on the delivery list for the next chocolate egg. However, it also had a setting that had never been used before. The Easter Bunny went into the settings and set to 'Best Kid in the world'. This was a setting that as it sounded would return the very best child in the world, most deserving of chocolate and also their address.

The Easter Bunny smashed the button with his hand and it made a few noises before returning the name "Hunter" and then showed the address of where they lived. On seeing the address the Easter Bunny told a group of eight Easter chicks to take him to visit Hunter as he needed to see them. After lifting him up high the chicks walked through a blue charged circular gate that instantly brought the whole team to Hunter's house.

The Easter Bunny had a detector that led him to Hunter's bedroom where he was currently playing with his toys. He then did something that the Easter Bunny has never done before…. He revealed himself to Hunter whom looked shocked and very surprised. After the chicks had calmed him down the Easter Bunny started to talk to Hunter and tell him of his predicament. After the story of the accident the Bunny looked Hunter in the eyes and said "Hunter, I need your help". "I need someone to deliver all the chocolate for me this Easter as I cannot move fast enough even with all the apps and gadgets we have. I need someone whom is very good and can keep secrets. Will you help?"

After a very short pause Hunter stood up and agreed to a pinkie finger promise with the Easter Bunny and the plan to save Easter had begun. Over the next few days Hunter was taught about all the skills needed to deliver chocolate and all of the gadgets that help him deliver and not be seen. The Easter bunny was impressed with his apprentice. So not to alarm Hunter's parents several Easter Chicks pretended to be Hunter whilst he was being taught which surprisingly seemed to work out well.

It was the night before Easter and Hunter sat with the Easter Bunny receiving last minute instructions. A timer in the corner clicked down until it said 'GO!'. Hunter pressed the ChoccoKidApp and began. Whizzing through the Blue circular gate at speed over and over again with batches of chocolate eggs. This was all done at such a pace as Hunter had been fed some magical chocolate from the Easter Bunny's own supply. The deliveries went on for hours and hours, until just before all the children were due to awake the deliveries were complete.

"Hunter – you've done it – you have saved Easter!" said the Easter Bunny who was crying with happiness. He was so thrilled and excited. All of the children throughout the world woke up to chocolate eggs the following day and everyone was happy. Hunter of course was tired and wanted to go to bed. He hugged the Easter Bunny and all of the chicks and headed off through the blue gateway one last time.

"To Hunter. Thank you for saving Easter and being the best human friend an Easter Bunny can have. Here is a special gift for you , but please don't eat it all at once as it is very special chocolate!"

Right there in his bedroom was the biggest chocolate Egg that anyone had ever seen, made from the Easter Bunny's own special formula which gives non-stop energy and takes away tiredness.

After one bite of the huge chocolate egg, Hunter's memory of his adventures with the Easter Bunny had vanished (along with the note) and all that remained was an energetic boy whom wanted to go outside and play and have an easter egg hunt. He loved Easter and loved chocolate. He loved his family so much as they loved him. Happy Easter to everyone and if you have lots of chocolate filled energy today then it's quite possible, if not highly likely that you were helping the Easter Bunny last night but just can't remember it any more!

Happy Easter from The Easter Bunny!

P.S. Thanks for Helping the Easter Bunny this year

Made in the USA
Monee, IL
11 May 2022

96208053R00017